THIS WALKER BOOK BELONGS TO:

_____

_____

_____

_____

First published 1994 by
Walker Books Ltd
87 Vauxhall Walk
London SE11 5HJ

This edition published 1996

2 4 6 8 10 9 7 5 3

© 1994 Julie Lacome

This book has been typeset in Monotype Bembo.

Printed in Hong Kong

British Library Cataloguing in Publication Data
A catalogue record for this book is
available from the British Library.

ISBN 0-7445-4382-7

I'm a Jolly Farmer

Julie Lacome

WALKER BOOKS

AND SUBSIDIARIES

LONDON • BOSTON • SYDNEY

I'm a jolly
farmer,
Here's my
horse and cart.

Giddy up,
horsy!
It's time to
make a start.

I'm a smiling princess,
An elephant I ride.

My throne is
perched
on top of him –
I'm glad his
back's so wide!

I'm a wildlife
warden,
I've tracked
this lion here.

He looks as though
he's fast asleep
But I won't
get too near!

I'm a deep sea diver,
I've met a dolphin friend.

We swim an
underwater race –
She beats me
in the end.

I'm Little Red
Riding Hood,
My granny's
ill in bed.

"What big teeth you have!" I say. I wish I hadn't come today…

I wish I'd stayed
at home to play…

With Fred!

MORE WALKER PAPERBACKS
For You to Enjoy

Also illustrated by Julie Lacome

WALKING THROUGH THE JUNGLE

"An absolute delight… Quite brilliantly, the artist has caught the slightly apprehensive air of the exploring child. As with the best of early years books, there is so much here to look at, to talk about and happily to share." *Children's Books of the Year*

ISBN 0-7445-3643-X   £4.99

SING A SONG OF SIXPENCE

Fifteen favourite nursery songs, including *Twinkle, Twinkle Little Star, Hush-a-bye Baby, Baa Baa Black Sheep* and, of course, *Sing a Song of Sixpence.* Each illustrated in bright, torn-paper illustrations that sing off the page!

ISBN 0-7445-5427-6   £4.99

A WAS ONCE AN APPLE PIE

A vibrant edition of the classic nonsense alphabet.

"Bright lively illustrations… The smallest toddler will respond to the sounds of this book." *The Daily Telegraph*

ISBN 0-7445-3146-2   £3.99

Walker Paperbacks are available from most booksellers, or by post from B.B.C.S., P.O. Box 941, Hull, North Humberside HU1 3YQ

24 hour telephone credit card line 01482 224626

To order, send: Title, author, ISBN number and price for each book ordered, your full name and address, cheque or postal order payable to BBCS for the total amount and allow the following for postage and packing: UK and BFPO: £1.00 for the first book, and 50p for each additional book to a maximum of £3.50. Overseas and Eire: £2.00 for the first book, £1.00 for the second and 50p for each additional book. Prices and availability are subject to change without notice.